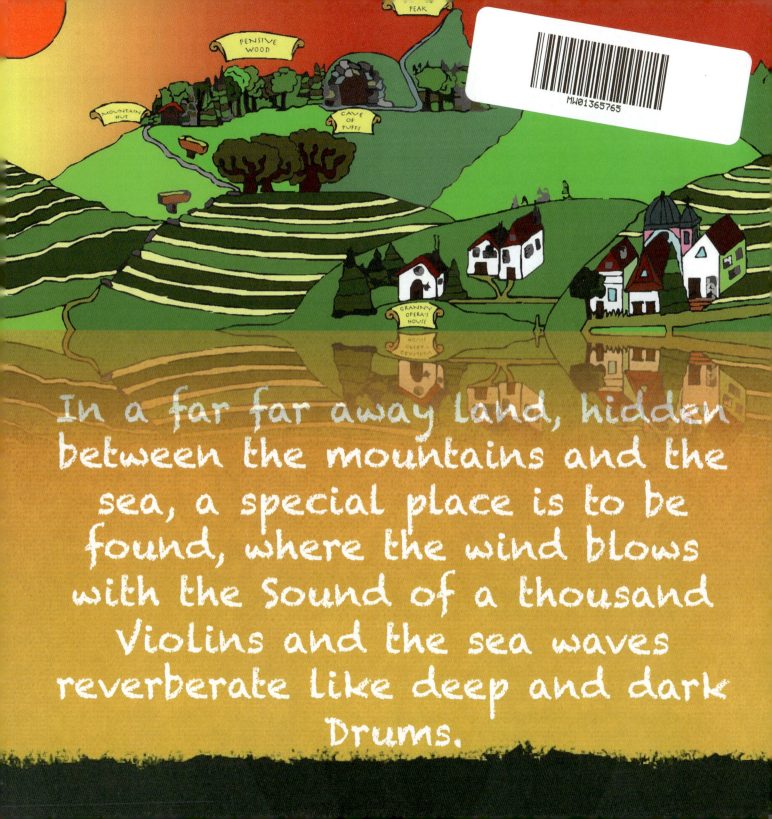

In a far far away land, hidden between the mountains and the sea, a special place is to be found, where the wind blows with the Sound of a thousand Violins and the sea waves reverberate like deep and dark Drums.

This place goes by the name of Sharpmountain.
There lives a friendly little lady, who loves listening to very loud music. Her name is Granny Opera.

On a very special evening she realizes that the moment has come. Her grandchildren Nota, Melodica and Armonia

have reached the right age to be told the oldest legend of Sharpmountain, the legend of Whiff the Elf.

Granny Opera approaches the bookshelves laden with ancient books

and with the three children looking on curiously, she pulls out a giant volume raising a cloud of black and white dust made of Notes.

At last she sits down, opens the book, puts on her spectacles and starts reading: The story tells that our Woods are inhabited by Elves. One of them, Whiff the Elf,

was a solitary one but also extremely brave: he longed to show everybody that he was capable of extraordinary things, so he meant to find the Clef of Happiness.

One day walking along in Pensive Wood he happened upon a cave. He didn't know at the time he was at the Mouth of the Cave of Puffs, a well-known dark place, from which dreadful Sounds,

that appeared to belong to a giant monster, came. All of a sudden an unbelievable force lifted him up and pulled him inside. He closed his eyes, terrified,

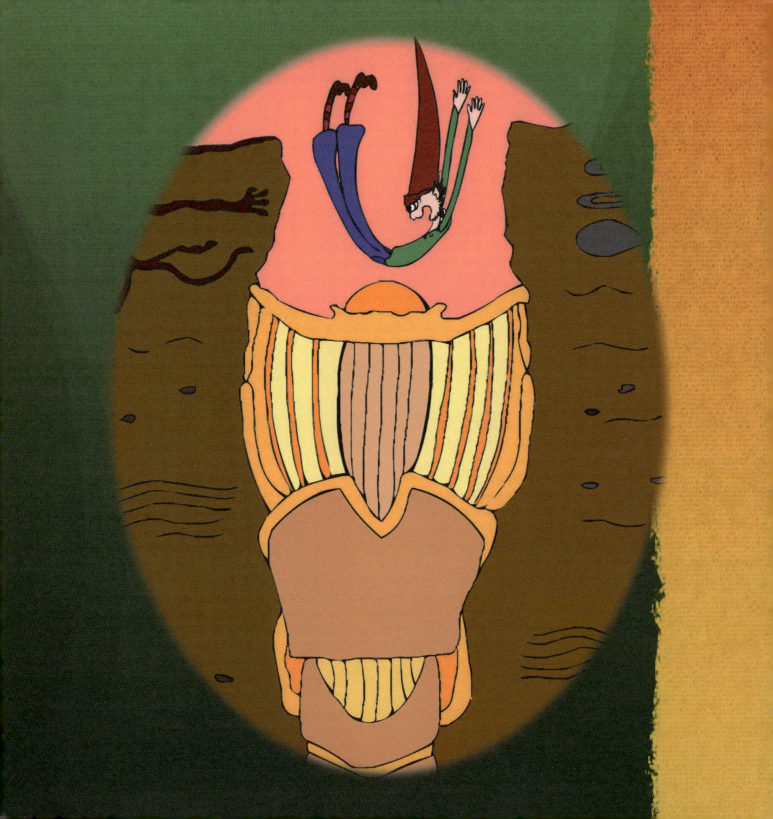

and when he opened them again he realized that the Cave was breathtakingly beautiful. He looked all around and he had the feeling of being in a huge pink tummy, with red and blue pipes, rivers and lakes.

Then he heard that loud, frightful, vibrating sound once more and he started running, till he got to the end of a tunnel: the beast was lying there, waiting for him. Whiff the Elf stood there motionless.

Before talking the Monster puffed and puffed: "Pfff, Pfff, Sssss ..." come closer little one" making a friendly gesture
"your presence tickles my nose, one of my sneezes would make you fly out of here in a flash. Step forward a little and make sure your tickling won't bother my nose. Pfff Pfff Ssss."

By now Whiff the Elf was paralysed with fear and as he thought he was coming to the end he did nothing, absolutely nothing. "Don't be scared, I won't do you any harm. What brings you here?? Pfff Pfff Ssss". Bronchus the Monster asked. Whiff the Elf timidly answered:
" ... the Clef of Happiness..."

"Well you've certainly come to the right place but you'll have to agree to be carried away by me in the presence of a few of my friends, and don't forget, the Cave of Puffs is where the Air becomes Sound! Puff, Puff, Sssss."

At that point Bronchus puffed once again while his Breath drove Whiff the Elf away but, still, Bronchus exorted the little Elf:

"Make a Sigh of Relief. Keep your chest wide open and your neck loose. Breath as Naturally as you can!"
So by that time he found himself right in front of Heart the Sorcerer who was playing his Drum:

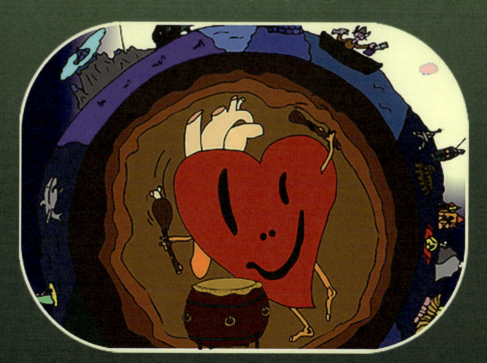

"Tu-tum, Tu-tum, Tu-tum...how can I help you my friend?"

Whiff the Elf, spellbound by the Rhythm, was not able to answer and Heart the Sorcerer smiled at him: "If what you're looking for is the Clef of Happiness then you should open your heart and listen to it. That way you will learn how to Receive the Sound and acknowledge the Tempo. The Breathing turns into Rhythm." And beating the Drumhead of the Magic Drum he pushed him away.

It was then that he reached Phrammy's Den, who by then was sitting down amid the lakes of an astonishingly beautiful underground Cave:

"Come closer, I already know what you're looking for and I have a gift for you: The Board of Resonance. Allow yourself to be get carried away to the exit and go through the Enchanted White Ribbons".

Once there, a series of Waves of Sound will surround you and by then you will almost be at the end of your journey. Then you will have to ride the Perfect Wave on this Board which has the Clef of Happiness' Notes carved on it.

If you succeed you will sense something happening...but if you don't, you'll never find the entrance to the Cave of Puffs again...
are you ready?"

Whiff the Elf nodded imperceptibly and Phrammy took it as a "yes" then waving at him he spread himself flat on the Floor of the Den like a soft omelette:

"Good Luck, daring Elf!" Whiff the Elf was already flying as if a tornado was carrying away a feather.

The tunnel's pink and damp walls whizzed past him, till at the end of the tunnel he saw two White Chantribbons open up at full speed, creating a Vibration.

He instantly found himself riding on the Board of Resonance, surfing on the Perfect Wave. The most beautiful sound he had ever heard resounded a Voice,

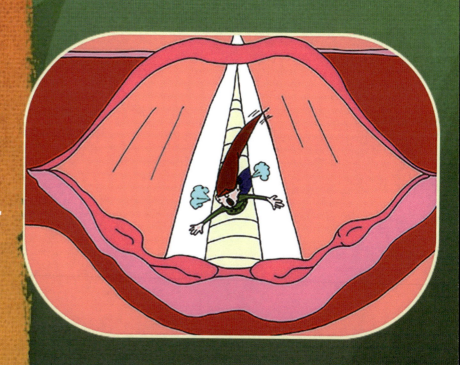

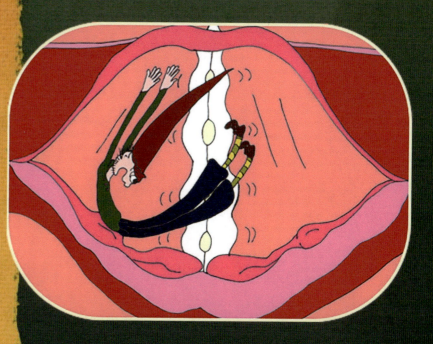

made of a thousand Harmonies and Choirs, like the magic of boundless colours and as beautiful as the wind.

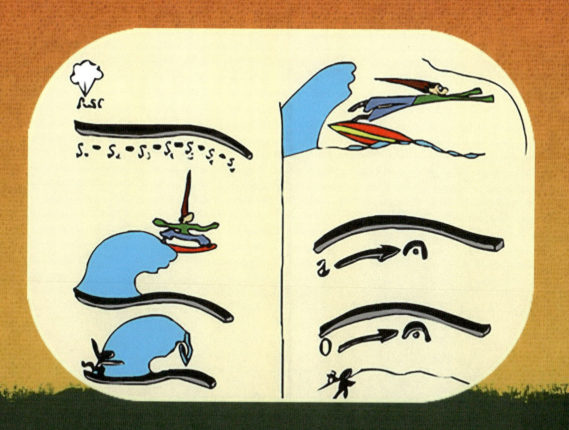

That Sound was nothing else but his own Voice and he was singing that one Note the same one carved on the Board of Resonance.
He felt elated.

Once he was outside he opened his hands and there was the Clef.

He could have shown it to everybody and boasted of having found it. But now that he had it, on the contrary, the only thing Whiff the Elf cared for was for everybody to be as happy as himself.

Granny Opera closes the big book knowing fine well that things would never be the same again for her grandchildren.

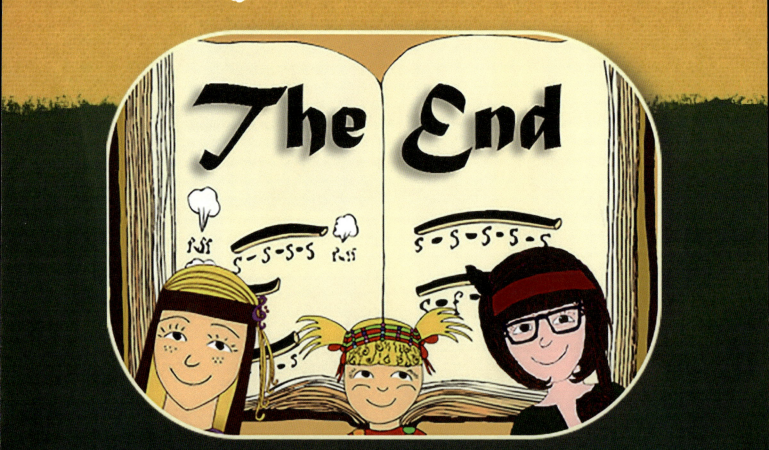

Written and illustrated by Elena Villa
Translated by Paola Mormone and Neil MacDonald Clunie

Made in the USA
Charleston, SC
15 February 2017